TORN BETWEEN A THUG & A BOSS

COMPLICATED LOVE SERIES BOOK 1

MIA BLACK

CHAPTER 1

Alivia

"Alright fellas, you already know what time it is!" said DJ Mercy. His booming voice came over the loudspeaker and filled the club. From behind the curtain I could see the lights starting to change colors. Green was my favorite color so I'd asked the owner of the club to make sure that there were green laser lights on me whenever I came out.

"We turned on the money green lights 'cause we need money on the stage. Coming to the stage next is Jade!"

DJ Mercy said my stage name and I turned into Jade, one of the highest paid strippers at the club. I came around the corner and parted the curtains, stepping out onto it and pausing. I looked around the men, their eyes all hungrily waiting for me to make my way down the long and narrow platform stage. The jet black sling-back heels that I was wearing were clicking and clacking as I did my sexiest walk towards the middle of the stage. I couldn't hear them over the sounds of the music playing

Before I hit the pole, I wanted to make sure that I had all the men's attention. I got down on the floor and started to crawl towards the pole, arching my back and poking my ass out. It was fat enough that it didn't need any poking but still. I got to the pole and put my back up against it, raising myself off the floor without using my hands and poking out my mid-section.

I turned around and wrapped my hands around the cold metal pole and slowly wrapped my leg around it as well. The lime green bra and thong that I was wearing would be off in a few minutes, but I needed to get the crowd even more excited first. I teased them at first, pretending to climb the pole and then not. Or, I'd spin around on it as if I was having the time of my life.

by the end of the night, he was asking me what I was doing when I left. I asked about his fiancée and it seemed like he'd forgotten about her.

"A bitch is tired," I said as I plopped down in the chair. I'd just walked to the back and was in the dressing room in front of my vanity mirror that I used to get ready before I went on stage. The dressing room was nicely decorated with gray lockers lining one wall and a long string of mirrors similar to mine lining the others. There neutral tan colored walls were decorated with rap album covers, something the owner thought was nice.

"You were working that little bachelor group, right?" Andrea asked. She was a natural beauty. 5'7" with super light skin, Andrea loved to have color in her hair. She was rocking a long burgundy wavy weave that complemented her skin. Guys loved looking at her curves but when she got up close to them they couldn't help but to compliment her on her beautiful face and full lips.

Andrea Lovelace was another stripper. More importantly though, she was my best friend, my rock, and the sister that I never had. The two of us had known each other since we were in high school. There was a funny story about how we met.

Andrea was a year older than me which meant that she was a year ahead of me in school. There was this cute basketball player name Ricardo that I had a crush on. He and I started talking to one another. Everything was cool for about a week or two. Next thing I knew, I found out that he had a girlfriend, Andrea. She ended up finding out about me as well. We were going to fight one another but instead we ended up jumping Ricardo for playing the both of us. It was funny to think about.

Andrea helped me out when I needed it the most. She was more of a sister to me than anything. We promised to always have each other's backs and we hadn't broken our promise yet. Growing up the way that I did, it was important for someone to look out for you, especially when your own parents couldn't do it themselves.

I was born and raised in Miami. The 305 was all I'd ever known but it was more than enough for me at times. It might sound nice to be from Miami. Most people only thought of South Beach or the downtown area. Sometimes

I wished I was from a nicer part of the city but there was nothing I could to change that. If you believed the movies and TV shows, you would probably think that all of Miami was like that: beaches, restaurants, frozen drinks, and parties. My Miami was different. Very different.

I was born and raised in the projects of Liberty City. If you were from Miami, you already knew what that was like. My neighborhood was one of those places that you knew you didn't want to be in when the sun went down, especially if you didn't know anyone. I lived with my mother, but I was pretty much raising myself. She'd been high on drugs for most of my childhood. It was sad, but the story was typical of a lot of people during that time. I didn't know who my father was. I wasn't even sure if my mother knew that. If she did she kept it to herself. At a certain point I just stopped asking because I knew that I wasn't going to get a real answer.

My mother wasn't a stable person at all back then. She had her own demons that she needed to deal with and used drugs to cope. I knew she loved me but at times she didn't express it the way that I felt she should have. As a result, I was in and out of the foster care system for most of my childhood. The last time I got out, I told myself that there was no way I'd be going back again. I'd run away from home or something before I let Child Protective Services show up and snatch me out of my home again. I learned to take care of myself. I figured out that the only way I was going to survive with everything that I had going on would be if I took things into my own hands, so I did.

It worked out in my favor that Andrea and I met and became cool. Her life was really similar to mine: single mother and no father in the picture either. I didn't realize it until we became cool, but she lived really close to me.

She might have only been a year older than me, but Andrea was wise enough for the both of us. She'd already seen the worst that the world could offer her and wanted to change it for the better. She was just like me. She'd made promises to herself that she planned on keeping. She made it clear that she was going to be in control of her own life. She wanted to move out of her house to take some of the burden off of her mother. That was what led her into the strip club. It had been a big shock to find out that she worked there. I was even more shocked when she told me that I should join her there.

Now, I'd joked about being a stripper before but had never actually been serious about it. I had to admit that I was one of those people who looked down on them at times. I didn't really understand why you'd get on a stage and take your clothes off for a bunch of thirsty ass dudes. Andrea explained to me that she was doing it because the money was fast and easy. She said that it would make it much easier for her to get out of her house.

I'd gone back and forth about it, but I ultimately made my choice and hadn't looked back ever since. Being young and pretty was a blessing and I was using it to my advantage. Andrea had only been there for a year longer than me, but it made all the difference. She showed me the ropes and taught me a lot. She taught me some moves which I made into my own. She told me how I should carry myself. Over time I developed my own skills and tricks and managed to shine on my own. We still made sure to watch out for one another at all times though.

"Yeah. I was doing it alone but when word

got out, there was a stampede of bitches coming to dance," I explained. "The good thing was that they weren't cheap. The groom was kind of handsome, but I don't think the marriage is gonna last though."

"Why not?" Andrea asked as she reached into her bag and pulled out a pair of jeans to change into. I hadn't seen much of her that night and I assumed she'd made good money because of it.

I laughed to myself. "Girl, that man was all up on me." I started imitating his deep voice. "What you doing after this? I'm only a free man for a few more hours. I can make it worth your while. Come on, nobody gotta know." I started to laugh.

Andrea busted out laughing alongside me. "I can't with these dudes," she chimed in. "So what did he do when you turned him down?"

I shook my head. "You already know how that goes. He moved onto the next bitch. He'll find somebody tonight, I'm sure. You know how some of these hoes are; dick and dollars go hand in hand."

Andrea shrugged. "Well, just be glad you ain't the one marrying him," she laughed.

Andrea and I finished changing our clothes and headed out to my car. The two of us lived together in a nice, two-bedroom apartment close to Downtown Miami. We figured it would be easier to have a nicer spot if the two of us split the rent. Each of us were usually in high demand at the club and were always getting booked for special events and private parties so rent and bills were never too much of a concern for us. We were smart about how we spent our money.

"You got class tomorrow?" I asked Andrea as the two of us walked into our apartment and turned on the lights. We were greeted to the scene of our nice sized living room with a huge couch and 55-inch TV on the wall. We'd decorated it together and it had come out nice. We'd agreed to paint the walls a light shade of gray and got colorful furniture to brighten it up.

Andrea walked over the couch and pretended to pass out as she laid down face down on it. "Just one and thankfully it's not until the afternoon," she said with relief. "I'm exhausted. I'll be glad when I don't have to do this anymore."

Something that I liked about Andrea and

something that we had in common with one another was the fact that we were both ambitious. The only difference was that she'd already figured out what she was passionate about and I was still trying to figure it out for myself. She was using the money that she made at the club to pay the rest of her tuition. She was in her final year of college and had been trying to land an internship at a magazine since her major was journalism. I knew that it was something that she cared about a lot, so I always made sure to support her.

"I feel like a walking zombie or something. I'm about to head to bed. See you in the morning," I called to her as I made my way down our short hallway towards my bedroom.

"Goodnight," she replied. I was pretty sure she was going to fall asleep right there.

The next morning, I got up bright and early. I tried to sleep in, but it never really worked out well for me. I headed to the bathroom to wash up and then headed into the kitchen to make myself some breakfast: oatmeal with fresh fruit. I prided myself on being in shape, so I tried to eat healthy as often as I could. I didn't want to be one of those people who got made fun of for being on stage and not looking my best.

"AHHHHHHHH!" Andrea's scream scared the mess out of me. The door to her bedroom burst open and she came down the hall with another scream, this time closer to my face. She was grinning like the Cheshire cat and I could tell she was excited.

"What happened?" I asked. "You alright?"

"Bitch I'm better than alright. I got the internship!" she exclaimed. She started jumping up and down with joy. I stood up and hugged her while I celebrated along with her.

"Oh my God! I'm so happy for you!" I gushed. "And you had the nerve to think they'd pick someone else over you."

"Thank you," she said as she took a seat. "I'm so damn excited."

"So, tell me about it? When do you start? Is it paid?" I questioned her. I was really happy because I knew that she'd been looking for something like this for a while.

"I start on Monday. It says that it's paid but only in a stipend. I can't really complain though. I'm just glad that I got it. You know how good this is gonna look on my resume when I graduate and start looking for jobs?" She was beaming.

"We should go out to celebrate," I suggested. "I wasn't planning on going to Tease tonight anyway."

"Me either. This works out perfect. You wanna pick the spot?" she asked.

"No problem. I heard about this place that just opened close to South Beach. We can go there," I said.

"I'm down."

Around 12:30 that night, Andrea and I were outside of the club and getting out of our cab. It was a Friday night, so we expected the club to be live. The line that was already there was crazy. I didn't know if there was a celebrity or something in town, but the people were trying hard to get in.

"Imagine if we had to stand on that line," Andrea said as she stifled a laugh. We walked towards the front of the club and straight to the promoter. I'd gone ahead and gotten us a table so that we wouldn't have any problems. It also helped that we knew the promoter because we'd worked with him before doing some private events.

Andrea and I made our way inside. I could feel the eyes of the guys around me, but I ignored it. I'd opted for a white dress that I purchased from some boutique online. It was a white wrap dress that was classy but still sexy at the same time. The silky material hugged my curves and showcased my cleavage but still left a lot to the imagination. Andrea also looked good, opting to wear a black dress with a long slit that showed off her thick thighs and long legs.

We sat down at our table and poured out some of the champagne that had come with it. As I looked around the large room, I could see why there were so many people outside waiting to get in. The club was already packed, and it looked like everyone was having a great time. The DJ was going off with the latest music and the dance floor and bar were packed.

I looked off to the left-hand side and saw a group of guys sitting in another VIP section. One of them in particular caught my attention. I couldn't see him up close since he was so far but from what I *could* see, he was handsome, muscular, and chocolate brown.

I sipped on my champagne and nudged

Andrea. "Who's that?" I subtly nodded my head in the direction of the group in the other VIP.

Andrea turned her head slightly and then looked back at me. "I've heard about him," she said. "His name is Dylan."

"So what's his story?"

"He's a boss," Andrea said. "And not like the rest of these play play niggas either. He's the real deal."

CHAPTER 2

Dylan

"Yo, let me get another two bottles of champagne," I said to the waitress.

"And some Henny," said one of my boys. I nodded my head in his direction and turned back to her.

"And some Hennessy," I added to her. Her eyes lit up. She probably figured that with all the money that I was dropping that she was going to get a really nice tip when we finished up. She was right too, as long as she kept the bottles flowing the way that I wanted them to.

"Anything else?" she questioned. I shook my

head. She nodded and turned to walk away, disappearing into the crowd of the club.

It was Friday night and the club we were at was packed. South Beach was always like that when the weather was nice, and that was most of the time. I was there to party with a couple of people from my crew, the inner circle for the most part. They'd finally be able to convince me that we should all take some time off to unwind and blow off some steam. There were about 7 of us in total, plus a couple of women. I swear it seemed like some of them came with the VIP section.

When we walked in the club it was easy to tell that we had money. We weren't flashy about ours or anything like that, but we definitely carried ourselves in a certain way. Not to mention the fact that we'd been ordering bottles of liquor like they were going out of style. After about an hour or so, the chicks started making their way over to us. We ended up letting the ones who looked the best into our VIP section. They probably thought they were running game on us or something, but we already knew what was up. They were partying and drinking with us to see which one of them could get a nigga for the night and hopefully get a couple of dollars out of it. It was regular Miami shit.

If there was one thing my city knew how to do, it was throw a party. The club was on tilt that night and there wasn't even a celebrity there. It just seemed like people came because they wanted to have a good time. The DJ was going in with the music, playing all the latest club songs and mixing in the classic throwbacks too. I didn't dance or anything, but I was on my feet most of the night with a bottle in my hand, rapping lyrics or doing my two step to the beat. One of the chicks who'd made her way into our section was doing her thing in front of me. Her ass was fat and all, but she was doing a little too much. It was clear she was working extra hard on me, trying to throw the pussy at me. She was pretty and all, but I didn't know if I'd take the bait yet.

Don't get me wrong, I could have hit it if I wanted to. I never planned on getting married and I wasn't in a relationship either. In fact, my situation was just the opposite. The issue was that I could spot a gold digger coming from a mile away and I'd seen girls like her before all the time. To her I was a target, so it was my goal to make sure that I didn't get caught up in any bullshit. I'd been paying attention to her all night and peeped how she was scoping out my watch and jewelry. They were shining though, so it wasn't like it was easy to ignore it.

Whenever I went out to a club or anything like that, I always tried extra hard to have a good time. The reason for that is that I didn't really have shit to celebrate when I was growing up. Now I was in a position where I could go ahead and ball out like it was my birthday even when it wasn't. When I was a kid I couldn't do that. Hell, I couldn't even imagine *having* the amount of money that I spent nowadays. I'd definitely come a long way.

My life was hard growing up. I couldn't lie about that if I wanted to. My mother, may God rest her soul, was a single parent like pretty much everyone that I knew then. I only had a handful of people that I knew who had both of their parents at home, and even then they usually fought all the time or something. My father wasn't around for us growing up. I realized at a young age that I couldn't worry about that. My mother told me some shit about how he'd run off with some other woman when we were young. I stopped asking about him after that. No man should ever leave his family behind. I promised my mother that she'd be alright because she had me and my little brother, Derrick, and that I'd take care of us.

The projects of Carol City don't love nobody. I learned that lesson growing up. I was always small for my age. Even now at 25, I hadn't reached six feet. I wasn't one of those dudes who felt insecure about their height though. If anything, being shorter made people want to try to pick on me more and I liked it. I hit the gym early to make sure that my body was getting stronger so people knew not to mess with me.

Dudes also tried me because they called me a mama's boy. I couldn't deny it. My mother was my heart. They didn't know how much she struggled to keep a roof over me and my brother's heads or keep clothes on our back. Watching her scrape together whatever money she could to make sure that we were good only made me want to help her out even more. It eventually got the point where people knew better than to say any of the stuff they said about me to my face. After a while, I learned that sometimes you had to *make* people respect you. That was what got me into the game.

I would never forget the first time I hit the block. I was a scrawny ass 12-year-old with a serious face. Around my way there were a couple of OG's who ran things. It was definitely on some old school shit. They looked out for people and helped out when they could, stuff like that. They also sold all the weight in the neighborhood and beyond. I knew a couple of them from around the way and I finally got one of them to put me out there.

The dude's name was Sammy D. He knew my mother and how much he struggled so I think he wanted to throw me a bone. I got started by being a lookout. There was nothing to it. I was basically getting paid to ride around on my bike and whistle or yell if I saw the cops coming. It went on like that for a while until I started proving myself more and more and Sammy took notice. He started moving me up slowly.

He taught me everything I knew about pushing weight. I moved up to being a corner boy, selling little nickels and dimes of whatever. After a while, that corner became my own and soon after that I had my own block. By the time I turned 20, Sammy had gotten killed and I was in the position to be the big boss. I had to crack a couple of skulls because people mistook my youth for inexperience, but it worked out for me. Five years later and I was still on top. My organization ran things around Miami. If you were moving weight, I knew about it 'cause you were probably doing it for me. My name definitely rang bells, so much that I'd get shoutouts from celebrities and athletes 'cause they knew that if they wanted certain things to happen that they needed to go through me.

Making my way to the top wasn't easy. Staying there was even harder. I always had to be on guard. A threat could come in the form of a chick trying to scam you to some random in the club who was jealous cause you looked like you had a lot of money. One thing that I could say for sure was that I'd *earned* everything that I had. It may not have all be gotten through legal means, but it was mine all the same.

When I first got into the game I tried to hide it from my mother and brother. It was easy at first because I was only making enough to buy a few groceries here and there. I honestly didn't want to disappoint my mother or brother. I knew that she was working hard and he'd always looked up to me. He was a couple of years younger and always tried to be like me. I figured that it was easier to keep them in the dark about what I was doing until I was old enough to get out on my own and then it wouldn't matter.

You know what they say: what's done in the dark always come to the light. By the time I hit 16 years old I was through pretending to be something I wasn't. I'd dropped out of high school. My mother long suspected what I was doing. One night when I got home late, she was sitting in the living room in the darkness. I came home and turned the lights and found her sitting there with my shoebox full of money in front of her. I'd been giving her money for a while but this was more than anything I could explain. There were stacks of all kinds of bills in rubber bands. I knew it hurt her when I explained what I was doing but she told me that she just wanted me to be safe and to at least finish school, so I went back and got my GED the next year just for her.

The next two years were honestly a lot easier than I thought they'd be. My mother never supported me selling drugs, but she knew that she couldn't stop me even if she tried. She didn't ask questions usually just let me be. I just naturally started taking care of the bills around the house to ease her burden.

I was thrown for a loop when I was 18. My mother died. Even now, years later, that shit still hurt me. She had a heart attack suddenly and was gone. The doctors couldn't even understand it because she was so young, but I figured she'd worked herself to death trying to make sure we were good. It was stress on her part. She didn't have any life insurance, but I'd been saving up my money, so I was able to bury her. After that. I ended up taking custody of my little brother. I knew that she wouldn't want him to end up like me, so I made sure that he got up and went to school every day. I also sent him away to school. Whatever financial aid didn't pay, I took care of. It was what my mother would have wanted for us.

It was a lot to balance, trying to halfway parent him and fulfill my commitment to the streets. I did it though. I learned how to balance and I taught myself a couple of lessons along the way. I made sure that Derrick was always good and that no one bothered him for anything. I also learned to rely on my closest friends because they'd been there for me and had never done me wrong in all the time that I knew them. That was why I brought them with me wherever I went.

"So papi, what you got going on after this?" The chick who was dancing in front of me turned around to face me. She looked like she was Spanish. I remembered she said that she was Cuban but every chick in Miami claimed to have some Cuban in their blood. I couldn't deny that she was pretty though. She had honey blood hair and lightly tanned skin. Her hair was long and came down past her shoulders. Not to mention that she had thick hips and a nice ass.

"What *you* got going on after this?" I countered. I decided to play along with her for a little bit. She stepped closer to me, so close that her breasts were rubbing against the fabric of my shirt. I didn't know what type of perfume or body oil she was wearing but it smelled like coconut.

She laughed a little bit. She was shorter than me, so she tiptoed up to whisper in my ear. "I'm with whatever you want," she said. Her hand briefly rubbed on the crotch part of my jeans. "Maybe a nightcap at your spot or something."

"We'll see," I said in a slightly flirtatious way. Now that she was doing all that extra shit, I was getting a little turned on. I knew she was excited because it seemed like she was catching the bait. Little did she know that I was never pressed for pussy. I always had a couple of different options for who I could smash whenever I wanted to.

When it came to women, relationships, and everything that fit under that umbrella, I had a different mindset than most. With the life that I lived, I couldn't be tied down. Women could be a headache and a burden at times. Beyond that, I wasn't one to be reporting my whereabouts or to have someone else questioning me about what I was doing and who I was doing it with. The less that some people knew, the better. I figured that there was an easier way to do things and I'd found it. I'd never been faithful in a relationship before, but I found a way to get around that that worked for me.

Being 25 years old, I considered myself a young nigga with an old soul. I'd seen and done a lot of things over the years. Standing at 5'11", my chocolate brown complexion had always earned me compliments from people who wanted to know how I kept my skin so clear. I'd always been small for my age, so I made sure that I worked out to develop my body just the way that I wanted it. Now I finally had the abs and everything that I wanted. I went to the barber faithfully every week to keep my line on point. Ladies fell for my dimples and strong jaw. I'd often been told that I could be a model. Add to that the fact that I was a boss, and you had the perfect recipe for bitches to throw themselves at you.

As I moved up in the world, I learned that I had to be smart about mine. I was thankful that I had Sammy there when I first hit the streets. He wasn't selfish with information like a lot of other dudes I knew. He made sure to tell me everything that he could. As he put it, he had a responsibility to put someone else on the same way that he'd been put on. He didn't just teach me about the game; he taught me about life. I guess you could call him my father figure.

I knew that as I climbed up the food chain there would be people with their hands out. I knew that a lot of chicks probably took one look at me and saw me as their meal ticket. I'd also seen time and time again how much of a liability relationships and attachments could be. For those reasons and more, I'd avoided relationships like the plague. The ones that I had let myself get into ended up being kind of a mess so I just stayed away from them in general. Instead of letting myself get locked down, I locked down a couple of women. I kept them.

"Keeping" women was something that I picked up from Sammy. I was impressed when I was a little dude because he always had the baddest bitches around him. The crazy thing was that he would mess with a few of them and they all knew about one another and were cool with it. Shit like that was something you only saw in the movies or if you knew a pimp in real life.

A "kept" woman, at least to me, was a chick that I was dealing with that I felt was worthy of keeping around. All the women that I kept had similar qualities. First of all, they all looked like models. Pretty faces, banging bodies, the whole nine yards. In order for them to be kept, they had to be cool with my rules. If they were with it, I'd put them up in a nice apartment or condo and took care of them. I'd see each of them a few times a week and chill, sex or whatever, depending on my mood and what I wanted in the moment. It might not make sense to many, but it did to me.

On the one hand, the women that I kept got everything they wanted without any of the hassles of a regular relationship. They got it all, hair and nails done. I took them out when I could. I threw them each some cash and told them they could spend it how they wanted with no questions asked, as long as they didn't ask for anything more. I wasn't too much like Sammy though, because I made sure to keep them all separate. That way there was way less of a chance for drama.

I wasn't out there trying to be Daddy Warbucks or anything like that, so it wasn't like all of them were staying in luxury condos like mine. I did make sure that they got set up in a spot that I had the key to and that their bills were taken care of. All they needed to do was make sure that they followed the guidelines that I'd set in place. It was nothing crazy, just rules to make sure that they could stay kept. If they broke the rules, I got rid of 'em. No questions asked. It definitely worked out for me because I guaranteed myself that I wouldn't have any problems with them.

Keeping the women in the cribs that I did also served another benefit. You had to be smart about the drug game, smarter now than ever before. With technology being the way that it was it would be easy to get caught up in something financial if you weren't careful. Between bank records and now all the different apps and stuff that we could use to send money, it was getting harder and harder to stay ahead of things. That's why I made sure that I took care of the money side of things through several different business ventures.

The apartments that my women stayed in were a part of my hustle. I had my name on all the leases but had put their names down as roommates with leases that I could terminate when I wanted to. If anyone came around asking about things, it would just look like I was into real estate. I made sure that I wasn't limited in what I did either. I purchased a small electronics store as well as a clothing store. Both of them were legitimate streams of cash coming in that I could use to clean my money. The electronics business was especially cool because I could ship my product right alongside the TVs and sound systems.

My real base of operations was out of one of the strip clubs that I owned. It was easy to launder money there 'cause everyone paid cash for everything. Club Silk was my main club, the biggest of the few that I owned. I was there all the time because I kept my office upstairs there. It made it easier to operate out of there because it was in a central location to everything.

My guys and I stayed at the club basically until it closed. We kept the liquor flowing and the party just kept on moving. I was glad that they'd been able to convince me to take the night off. When it was over and we headed outside for the let out, the chick I'd been dancing with all night ended up coming outside with us. She was a little tipsy and I could admit that I was too. I hadn't just been holding onto those champagne bottles, I'd been pouring them.

I knew it was a little fucked up, but I'd forgotten her name. I tried to think of it again but when I couldn't, I ended up just blurting out the question.

"It's Marisol," she said seductively. She

didn't seem to have an attitude or anything like that. My crew was already starting to pile into their cars. I saw some of them had a female on their arms that they hadn't gone into the club with.

"Oh yeah, I remember now," I said.

She put her hand on her hip gave me a seductive look "So, what you wanna do, papi?"

She poked her breasts out a little more. I looked her up and down again and decided to just roll with it. I'd throw her some cab fare in the morning plus a little extra, but that was about it. She wasn't the keeping type.

CHAPTER 3

Alivia

Going out with Andrea had been a lot of fun. We were still on a high from the good news of her internship, so we had a really good time. I didn't really get a chance to go out too often. The club ended up taking most of my evenings, so it was always nice when I got a chance to get out and just be myself. We stayed till about an hour or so before the club closed and then headed to a 24-hour diner to grab some food and sober up a little bit before we went home.

I worked at Tease over the weekend and made some good money. Working at the club I could usually tell the vibe whenever I walked in. Saturday the club was packed. I'd forgotten about it until I got there but some rapper was in from out of town and was having an event that night. I hit the stage of course and ended up making serious cash. A couple of dudes from his entourage tried to get at me but I turned them down. Sundays were usually either hit or miss. It was slow, so I just focused on getting in a couple of lap dances before I went home for the night.

"Can you pass me my bag?" Andrea asked. I reached over to the bed and handed it to her while she stood in front of the mirror. She was dressed in a lime green bra and panties set with matching garter.

"How many people are supposed to be out there?" I questioned her. It was Monday evening and we were working a private event.

Andrea had been at the first day of her internship all day long, but when she got home that day she told me about how much she'd enjoyed it. She said that she was really excited about graduation because it meant that she could find something else to do besides stripping, hopefully something in the career path that she'd chosen for herself. I was glad that my girl was doing something that she felt passionate about.

About a month prior, I'd been approached by this guy after giving him a lap dance. He was white and also the white-collar type. He turned out to be a lawyer, just as I'd assumed. He explained to me that he was looking for a couple of girls to dance at a party at a private residence. It was going to be a birthday surprise for one of his friends. I told Andrea about the opportunity and we agreed to do it together.

Private events could mean a lot of different things. Most of the time people wanted us to work the same types of events. Things like bachelor and birthday parties were the usual. Sometimes club promoters would come by the club looking for a few women just to be present. It raised the profile of the club if people knew that beautiful women went there.

Working private events with Andrea always put me at ease. We didn't have to worry about who was getting the biggest cut because we split the money evenly. I knew that she had my back and I had hers. If we felt bad vibes or anything we'd always leave or make sure that we had a weapon ready in case anything popped off. We weren't expecting any of that from a room full of white guys in business casual wear though.

We both finished getting dressed. I'd opted to put on all red everything: bra, panties, garters, and even my heels were red. It definitely made my blonde hair stand out even more. I looked dressed to kill, literally. I was working an image that night, so I'd brought a pair of hand-cuffs with me as well. I only planned on danc-ing, but guys usually liked it when the whole image was put together.

There was a knock at the door and the guy who'd invited us, Matthew, asked if he could come in. I told him yes and he stepped inside.

I had to laugh to myself once he got inside. Men were so obvious sometimes. Whether they were the CEO or the janitor, they had one thing in common, they all loved pussy and looking at beautiful women. No sooner than he came into the room, Matthew's eyes were all over us. I damn near told him to take a picture because it would last longer. I knew we were nice to look at, but he'd be seeing more of us in a little while.

"Are you ladies ready?" he asked the two of us. He was dressed casually in a pair of light blue jeans with a white button-down shirt with the sleeves rolled up. His black shoes were simple but expensive.

"A few more minutes and we should be good," I said. I wanted to make sure that my makeup was touched up before I stepped out. "Is the birthday boy here yet?"

Matthew smiled and nodded. "Yeah, and he has no idea you guys are coming to surprise him," he explained. "He's gonna love it. Can I get you something to drink?"

"No, we don't drink during these things," Andrea answered for me. We didn't really drink at work or even during private events. Both of us enjoyed being aware of what was going on. It was sad sometimes to see the way that some of the other bitches in the club got. They'd take shot after shot and smoke a lot of weed just to get through. My thought was always along the lines of if you need this much to do it, maybe you just shouldn't. "Thanks for the offer though."

Matthew shrugged casually. "Alright, suit yourself, but there's a full bar downstairs if you get thirsty. Just shoot me a text when you're ready to come out and I'll come back to show you where you'll be."

I nodded my head at him before he turned and headed out of the room. Andrea finished getting dressed while I headed into the bathroom to make sure all my makeup was on and looking good. When we were both finished, I sent Matthew a text letting him know that we were ready.

He came upstairs a couple of minutes later and explained everything to us again. It was pretty standard. It was a birthday party, so we were just there to be eye candy. It all came down to smiling, looking good, and selling the fantasy that they could have us. He told us that he'd already spoken to the guys downstairs and let them know that they should tip. He also assured us that none of them were broke so we could expect to make a nice chunk of change. Once he'd finished detailing everything, he led us down the spiraling staircase towards the huge living room where the party was taking place.

I didn't know if it was his house or something that was rented for the night. Either way, the only word to describe it was lavish. It had a very modern feel to it with lots of black and silver items. There was also a lot of artwork on the wall, which was usually a sign of money. I was impressed and hoped to live like that someday.

"He's gonna love this," Matthew said eagerly. He turned to face us with another grin on his face. He was buzzing like a little kid who was finally about to get their desert. As we got closer to the room I could hear jazz music playing. That could be cool for after we danced, but it wasn't gonna work to take our clothes off to. I asked Matthew if he had anything else, so he ended up changing it before we got into the room. I wanted something that would lighten up the mood.

The guy whose birthday it was, Timothy, was sitting down in a chair in the middle of the room. I stepped inside and looked at the eager looks on the faces of the other guys around him. There were about 15 of them in total. They were mostly White but there were two Black guys and an Asian man as well. Their ages varied but it was clear that none of them were under the age of at least 35. Timothy looked like he was in his mid 50s.

"Alright fellas. What's this all about?" Timothy asked. He had a blindfold on so he didn't know that we'd joined them in the room.

There was a mid-tempo R&B song playing in the background. Andrea and I exchanged a look with one another as we tried to decide who would end up doing what. I nodded my head towards Timothy and she nodded.

Because Andrea and I were so close and had worked parties together before, we had a way of just knowing how we wanted to do things. There were two of us so while I danced for Timothy, she'd make her way around the room teasing all the other guys and then we'd switch. We did it because it was easier to get the guys to loosen up that way.

I'd put a tan trench coat on top of my outfit so all the guys could really see were my long, thick legs and a pair of heels. Andrea got started and walked up to one of the guys while I made my way over to Timothy. I pulled the blindfold off of his head and the look of pure shock on his face on his face as he looked at me and then my body almost made me laugh out loud.

"Oh shit," he said. "Damn, damn, look at you."

"Yes," I said as I leaned down and whispered in his ear, "look only at me. But don't touch."

I started my dance at that moment. I listened to the beat of the song playing in the background and moved my body to the beat. I propped my leg up on the chair and put my foot on his crotch. I straddled him and then lifted my leg over his body so I could turn my back to him. Every time he tried to touch me, I'd swat his hand away. I danced for him for a few minutes, grinding my hips and ass against every part of his body that I wanted to.

It was clear that my dance was working. Timothy was rock hard through his pants. He looked like he was about to jump out of the chair and tackle me, and I hadn't even taken off my coat yet. I looked at Andrea and she seemed to be enjoying herself as she moved from guy to guy. I nodded my head at her and the two of us switched off. She walked over to Timothy and I walked over to one of the Black guys that was there.

"Damn baby, what's your name?" he asked. He looked to be the youngest of the group but he gave off the energy of someone older. I noticed the wedding ring on his finger, not that I cared about it. I was there to sell a fantasy and that was it.

"Jade," I whispered seductively as I tiptoed to reach his ear. I undid the belt on my trench and then pulled it open to reveal my full outfit. The other guys in the room all started to come over to me once that happened.

"So, who's next for a dance?" I asked the small crowd of guys that had formed around me. All of their hands went up. In my head all I saw were dollar signs.

"Ladies, you did your thing!" Matthew came up to us as we were about to leave and head home. We'd already been paid for the night, so he'd just come to tell us goodbye.

"We aim to please," I said with a laugh.

"Was everything the way you wanted it to be?" Andrea asked. "Did Timothy enjoy himself?"

Matthew nodded. "Hell yeah! He's never gonna stop talking about it."

"That's what we like to hear," I said with a smile. "Call us if anyone else is having a party or something."

"Well, it's funny you should say that," Matthew said, "'cause I've got something you could do."

"What is it?" I asked. Matthew seemed cool,

so I hoped that he wasn't about to ask for sex or anything like that. It wouldn't be the first time a guy asked for a threesome with Andrea and me.

"There's a party happening this weekend that you should come to. I'm gonna be there and so will a lot of other people," he said.

"What kind of party?" Andrea asked cautiously.

"The expensive kind," Matthew said with a laugh to himself. "There's a private event happening on Star Island. I think a record label or something like that is throwing it. Either way it's gonna be a big deal. The best music and food. Celebrities. I even hear there's a dance contest and a best dressed contest."

"That does sound like fun," I commented. "What's the catch?"

"No catch," Matthew said with a shake of his head. "It's just an invite. If you can make it I think it'd be fun. I can email it to both of you. All you have to do is make sure you RSVP so your name can be on the list."

"Alright, sounds good," Andrea said. I could tell she was ready to go. Matthew took both of our email addresses and sent the invite right then and there before we headed back home.

Andrea and I talked it over in the car on the way home. The invite looked pretty legit, so we decided we would go and check it out. We made plans to go shopping the following day when she got off of her internship.

The next day, the two of us hit the mall just as we'd planned. There was a best dressed concert that paid $500 to the winner and it was the same for the dance contest. We bought new clothes for the concert plus some extra stuff.

It was a Tuesday so neither of us were heading into Tease that day. Instead, we stayed home and turned on some music. We came up with a dance routine for the contest at the party. Safe to say that we planned on winning the contest and impressing some people.

CHAPTER 4

Dylan

I was upstairs at Club Silk on the computer going over some of the books for some of the businesses that I owned. I knew that I wasn't the corporate type, but I loved my office. It was up on the second floor of the club and had a huge glass window that let me look out over the whole club. I liked being able to see everything that was going on.

When I first got into owning legitimate businesses, I hired a business manager to oversee them all. I was intelligent and able to pick up things quickly, but I didn't know enough to manage all of my different places on my own. Each place had its own individual management team and everything but the manager I'd hired, this dude in his mid 30s named Marcus, was the one who checked in on the places more frequently than I did to make sure that everything was running smoothly. Marcus was up on game so he knew what I was doing with the money. He got a cut outside of his normal salary for keeping his mouth shut about things.

Every now and then I liked to check in on things myself and see how it was going. I felt like it would have been stupid of me to just let Marcus and everyone else that worked for me just go on without thinking that I wasn't paying them any attention. People worked harder when they knew that the boss was close by and I was never too far away.

I headed into my email to check it. I saw that I'd been invited to attend an event that was taking place that upcoming weekend. The more that I networked with people and stuff, the more places I got invited to. I checked over the invitation to make sure that it wasn't anything bogus, but it seemed pretty legitimate. It would be at a private club over on Star Island. From what the invite detailed, it was gonna be an A-List only event.

I saw that the invite said dress to impress. It mentioned a dance contest that I knew I didn't care about at all. It also said something about a best dressed contest. I definitely wasn't about to enter a contest since I dressed to impress everywhere I went. Still, I decided I'd use it as a chance to pick out some new clothes and shit.

I pulled the chair I was in away from the desk and walked over to the couch where one of my right-hand guys, Slim, was napping. I tapped him roughly on the leg to wake him up.

"Wake up nigga," I said as I nudged him. "What's wrong with you? You pregnant or something? You been sleeping like a bitch all day."

Slim, just as his name implied, was tall and lanky. He'd always been that way for most of his life but he seemed to want to change all that because for the last few months he'd been working out in the gym trying to pack on some muscle. His deep caramel complexion and short curly hair had always been enough to get whatever woman he wanted, but he was tired of getting called skinny by everyone.

"Shut the fuck up," he grunted back as he cleared his throat. "I was up with Jasmine last night. I ain't see her in a while so you already know we had some catching up to do."

Slim and I went way back. He and I knew each other from around the way so it only made sense for me to take him with me to the top. He was one of the only people that I could say I trusted with my life.

"You done playing businessman?" Slim went on as he stood up to stretch. "What are you about to do?"

"I just got an invited to this party this weekend. It's supposed to be packed. Celebrities and women and shit. You know, the regular? You down to go?" I sat on top of my desk with my arms crossed waiting for his response.

Slim started to grin. "You know I'm with it. Let's get some of the crew and we can make a it a big thing."

I nodded my head. "Alright, sounds good. Look, I was about to head to the mall to get some new shit for the party. You wanna ride with me?"

"We out," he agreed.

Slim and I ended up meeting up with some

of the other members of the crew and we all headed to the mall together. I made sure that my people were well compensated financially so when we got to the mall, they were each able to ball out in their own way. I let them know what they could expect from the party so they all went and picked out something nice and dressy to wear that still fit their individual style.

I ended up picking up a couple of things. Some of it was options for the party but most of it was just stuff that I saw and wanted to have. That had kind of become my thing since I'd gotten money. When I was younger, if I saw something that I wanted, I already knew the chances of my mother being able to afford it were slim to none. If she did end up having some extra money or something, it usually went to bills and stuff for the house. I'd usually end up just telling her to get stuff for Derrick because he was younger than I was and didn't really understand why we couldn't afford nicer things.

When we were finished at the mall, I climbed into my truck with Slim and one of our other guys named Jerome. The three of us were heading back to Club Silk. I had to take a phone call with one of my suppliers. I usually did all of my business there.

Slim was driving while Jerome sat in the back. It was quiet, so I decided to use the time to check in one of the women I kept, this chick named Kira.

Kira and I had met each other a couple of months ago. It was funny because I met her in the last place that I could usually be found, a coffee shop. I'd stopped inside to try and use their bathroom. I was gonna leave when I was finished but I spotted this young, chocolate thing behind the counter so I stepped up to buy something.

I didn't know how old she was at the time, but I could tell she was young. I ended up getting her to write her number on my receipt. I ain't even have to spit a lot of game to get her fall for me. I was just charming like that.

We went out one or two times before I told her what was up. I explained what I saw in her and told her that I wanted to keep her. Being so young she had a lot of questions and shit but I told her that it was simple enough. Follow the rules and everything would be fine. She said that she didn't know about it since she was in school and working to pay her bills. When I told her that I'd help her with the tuition money that she needed, she was with it.

I pulled out my phone and dialed her number. She answered after a couple of rings.

"Hello? What took you so long to answer?" I asked as picked up the call.

"Why you always sound so mad?" Kira answered. "I'm sorry boo. I just got out the shower."

I looked over to Slim to make sure he wasn't all in my conversation. "Oh word? How was that?"

She laughed a little bit. "It was good. It would have been better if you were here with me. You coming to see me anytime soon? I miss you."

"I'll be there when I be there," I said in a serious way. I hated being questioned about places I'd been on be. Kira knew better then to ask me questions but every now and then she did it. She thought it was playful and I let it slide. "So what you do last night? I hit your line and ain't get a call back."

"What? What you talking about?" Kira's

voice sounded confused on the other end of the phone. "What time did you call?"

I sucked my teeth. "Don't play that dumb shit with me, Kira. You know exactly what time I called. The phone rang. I know you went out last night. Where'd you go?"

I had a list of rules that my kept women had to follow. I wasn't a slave master or anything like that, so they were free to come and go as they pleased, as long as they were available when I wanted them to be and didn't do anything dumb. Kira went out the night before and didn't come back until a little after two in the morning. I didn't know where she went but it definitely wasn't something that she'd told me about.

"Oh, nowhere," she said in a slightly high-pitched voice. "I was just hanging out with some of my girls."

"Till two in the morning? Must've been some girls' night," I commented.

"How you know what time I got in?" she asked nervously. "I was just hanging out with Jasmine and them." I damn near laughed when she said that. If she was gonna tell me a story she should have done her research first.

"Kira, you lying and we both know it," I

said. She didn't know that I had intel that said that she wasn't where she said she was. "My man saw you at the bar last night."

I could hear the panic in her voice as she tried to explain herself. "D, I swear it ain't even how you're making it seem. I was with Jasmine. You could even call her and ask her. I just hung out with my girls. We had a couple of drinks and that was it. Nothing crazy. Why don't you come over here so I can show you how sorry I am?"

I shook my head and raised my voice a little bit when I spoke to her. If there was one thing that I hated, it was a liar. She wasn't even a good one.

"Oh, so I could call Jasmine and she'd tell me what happened?" I played along with her.

"Yes," said Kira assuredly.

"That's funny to me," I said. "Cause Slim is right here and he said that he was chilling with Jasmine last night. So unless she got a twin that we don't know about, you're lying.

"Oh...." Her voice trailed off. "I promise you I didn't do anything funny. It was just a girls' night out."

"Don't try and play that shit off. I spoke to

you yesterday. Why ain't you say you was going out?" I questioned her.

"It was just a last-minute thing," she went on. "I wasn't even gone for that long. Don't be mad at me."

"You know my rules, Kira. You know I don't play that shit. You gotta go," I said coldly. "You clearly must not remember who I am."

There was real fear in her voice by then. "What you mean I gotta go? Dylan, can't we talk about this? Calm down. Let's be rational. It was just the bar. I ain't even dance with anybody."

"I don't give a fuck," I went on. "You're cancelled. I told you how it was when we first started chilling with each other. Don't act like you ain't know what would happen."

"So what? You're just gonna kick me out? What about all my stuff?"

"What stuff are you talking about?" I asked. "Cause everything in that apartment belongs to me. You can keep the clothes and shit but I want my jewelry."

"You just expect me to pack all this shit up and go? Where am I supposed to go, Dylan? I can't go back to my mother's house. She was mad when I moved out," Kira pleaded with me. I could hear her getting more and more emotional. "I'm sorry for not telling you where I went. You know you can trust me."

"Bitch, you're wasting your breath trying to explain something to me when you need to be using that energy to pack your shit up," I said in a loud voice. "Somebody is gonna be by later to make sure that you're out."

"What the fuck? I can't even get a few days to try and find somewhere else to go?" Kira sounded like she was on the verge of tears. I guess she was realizing how serious I was and what that meant to her future. "What the fuck am I supposed to do? You really just gonna drop me?"

"You should've thought about that before you broke the rules. No staying out all night, remember?" I asked her. She was silent on the other end of the phone as I hung up on her. She called me a few times and when I didn't answer she started texting me. At first it was her saying she was sorry. Then she was pleading with me to give her time to try and find a new spot. I told Slim to send a couple of the guys over to the spot to make sure she left and didn't do anything dumb like try damage something before she went. She was getting evicted whether she wanted to be or not.

We got back to the club a little while later. We were running a little late so by the time we'd gotten there, the two dudes that I was supposed to meet up with were already there.

Jean and Claude were these two Haitian dudes who ran Little Haiti in Miami. They were also my connects. The two of them were brothers and thick as thieves. I'd heard stories about some of the things they'd done to the people who'd crossed them. I wasn't afraid of them at all, but I knew to just be a straight shooter with the both of them. I didn't want to have to war with them for any reason, plus we made each other a lot of money so it was in everyone's best interest to keep things cool.

Jean and Claude had these thick ass Haitian accents which I had a hard time understanding sometimes. I always made sure to pay close attention to everything they said because I knew how much they hated having to repeat themselves. We ended up making plans for a couple of drops. I switched up the way I did things every now and then in case the police or anyone else was paying attention to me. Sometimes I liked to get all of my product in one big shipment. Other times I had smaller batches going to different places so it could get broken down into packs to move. I had to be smart about the way I did things.

I'd just about finished up with Jean and Claude when my phone started to ring. I would have ignored it but it was my brother. The two of us were incredibly close and spoke often so I excused myself so I could answer and see what he wanted.

"Yo? What's good boy?" I answered the phone.

"What's up bro? Nothing much. What are you up to?" Derrick's happy voice came through the phone. I loved my brother and was glad that I'd been able to save him from living the same life as me. Don't get me wrong, my brother wasn't a punk by any means. He'd fought and proven himself in our neighborhood on many occasions. He just wasn't built for everything that I was doing and that was fine with the both of us. His place was away at school, getting good grades and worrying about his white-collar future.

"You know me, always handling some business," I said. "What about you?"

"Just got out of class," he replied. "I just took a mid-term. It was easier than I thought it would be, but we'll see how that goes."

"You know you always ace them, so I don't know why you're second guessing it," I encouraged him. I wanted Derrick to do well for himself but also because it was what our mother would have wanted.

"Whatever," he mumbled. "So look man, what you got going on this weekend?"

"This weekend?" I remembered the party that I'd been invited to. "I got this invite to a party out on Star Island. Celebrity type shit, you know?"

I could practically hear him smiling when he spoke again. "Oh word? Well I was planning on coming home for the weekend and bringing my girl with me. You think we could roll with you?"

"Of course. No doubt," I replied. "Who's this girl? How long have you known her?"

"You think you my pops or something?" he joked. "Her name is Naomi. We have the same major. We've been talking for a couple of months now so I wanted to show her some of where I'm from."

"Oh word? You must be serious about her to be bringing her here, but it's cool. The more the merrier," I said.

"Alright. Sounds good," he said. He got quiet for a moment. "Um, you think I could stay at one of your places, bro? I was gonna get a hotel but I figured I'd ask."

"Nigga, that's not even a question. Hit me when you get here and I can take y'all out for lunch and give you the key to a spot," I said.

"Thanks D," he said. "I'm about to run to my next class but I'll call you a little later and see you Friday when I get in."

"Alright, sound good. Stay up," I said to him before I ended the call and headed back out to finish my business with Jean and Claude. I was feeling a little more excited about the party than before.

CHAPTER 5

Alivia

It was the night of the big party and Andrea and I couldn't have been more excited about it. All week long we couldn't stop talking about it. At work and at home, we talked about what we'd wear and tried to guess what celebrities would be there. A couple of the girls at the club hear us talking and asked about it. We explained that it was invite only and all of their faces dropped. I knew a couple of them would try and work their way inside if they could get the information, but I didn't see that happening. I'd been to parties where celebrities had been and stuff like that. It wasn't like I was the type to get star struck or anything like that. However, this private party with its invite only guest list seemed to be in a league of its own.

Andrea and I were in full on girls' night mode. We bought a couple of bottles of champagne and wine for the house. We wanted to sip on something while we got ready. We turned up some music and started getting ourselves together. According to the invite the party started at 10 so we planned on getting there a little before midnight. No one wanted to be the first one there, standing around looking dumb while waiting for more people to arrive. Plus, it would give us a chance to really make an entrance in our new dresses.

I still hadn't decided on an outfit for the party. When we went shopping I ended up buying a couple of different outfits to wear. I didn't know what kind of vibe I wanted to give off. Andrea was in the same predicament.

"Andrea!" I called out to her from my bedroom. "Can you come here real quick?"

She walked into my room a couple of seconds later, still wearing the same bathrobe that she'd had on twenty minutes earlier. Thankfully we'd started getting ready earlier than usual because we knew it would take us longer.

"What's going on?" She asked.

"I need your help. Pick between these two dresses," I said. I'd been going over everything in my closet for what felt like all day long. I'd finally narrowed my choices down to these two new dresses but couldn't choose between them.

She stared down at the two dresses and then finally spoke. "I like the green. I feel like money green is right for a night like this."

"I was thinking the green one too," I said. "Thanks. What do you mean by a night like this?"

"I don't know," she mumbled. "It just feels like it's gonna be a good night. You know? I've never been out there before but I've heard things. I think it's gonna be really fun."

"Me too," I agreed. "I'm glad that we can just be guests and don't have to work the event."

"Same here. Although, I know there's gonna be mad niggas with money in there, but I don't feel like dancing or working a crowd," she said. She started doing some of the little routine that we'd come up with. "Only dancing I'm doing is this."

I couldn't help but to laugh. She'd taken the dance and was doing it hard as though she was auditioning for a music video or something like that. "You're crazy. You know that, right?"

"Bitch so are you, why do you think we're friends? Come on and help me choose an outfit for myself," she said.

After I helped her pick out something to wear, the two of us finally started getting dressed. We had a lot of back and forth in each other's rooms because after the dresses, we helped each other out with hair, makeup, and choosing shoes and accessories. What were best friends for?

We had a huge floor length mirror in the living room close to the door. I'd just finished getting all the way ready and was standing in front of it checking out my outfit.

I was glad that I'd chosen the dress that I had. It was classy and elegant but still sexy. It had long sleeves and came down to just below my ankles, a little above the floor. There was a long slit in the front that showed off my legs and made me look taller. The front of it had a deep V-neck that met in a design in the middle. I was glad that my breasts sat up as much as they did because there was no way I could have worn a bra with an outfit like that. I'd put on gold heels with the dress and had made sure to only wear gold accessories as well. I'd put my hair up into a high ponytail to complete the look.

Andrea came out a couple of minutes later. She was wearing a gray dress that showed off all of her curves. She'd gotten her hair done earlier in the day so her weave was longer and fuller. She also checked herself out in the mirror.

"Bitch, we look like money!" Andrea gushed. She pulled out her phone. "Let's take a couple of pictures before we go." She started snapping pictures in the mirror, hitting all types of angles and things before we headed out.

We decided to take Andrea's car to the party instead of a cab. We figured it would probably be easier for us to get home if we did that. We drove out to the infamous Star Island with the radio turned up so we could get ourselves into the mood to party. We followed the directions and got out there quicker than we thought we would.

From the moment we arrived I could tell that the party was different than other ones that we'd been to before. There was a valet outside of this long walk way. He came up to us and took the car while directing us on where we should go. The both of us walked up the long, carpeted walkway towards the actual venue. Star Island was actually pretty small so mostly everything there was close to the water.

There was no line at the club. I hadn't been expecting there to be either. Not everyone knew about the party so it wasn't like the normal birds who went to things like this could get in.

The man at the door was big and built like a bouncer. He was way over six feet tall and looked like he was a solid muscle. He was dressed formally in a suit though and was sitting down behind a little desk with a computer on it.

"Hello ladies," he said. He smiled at us. "Names?"

I'd made sure to RSVP to the party and I'd printed out the invite just in case there was any trouble at the door.

"Alivia Conner and Andrea Lovelace," I told him. He looked down at the computer and pressed a few keys before looking back up at us. "Alright, you're both clear to enter. You didn't choose your entries though. Did you want regular or VIP service? Obviously VIP comes with a table and other amenities."

Andrea and I looked at one another and made a choice without saying anything. "We're gonna do the VIP," I said. "We just need a table and some champagne. It doesn't have to be a whole lot since it's just the two of us."

He smiled and typed away. "Alright, that'll be $500."

I pulled out my card and handed it to him before we went inside. A bottle girl met us at the next door to show us inside.

I had to admit that I was impressed. From the outside the club looked kind of outdated. The inside looked like it had been completely renovated. It was a huge space with two floors and a balcony at the top. The downstairs area had a huge area for dancing as well as a stage on the other side. There were several VIP sections and tables all around. On the downstairs floor there were a bunch of glass doors that we open that led right out onto the beach. It was very easy to tell that someone had put a lot of thought and effort into this place. The attention that they'd paid to detail was amazing.

Overall the atmosphere at the private club

was what really pushed it over the edge. When you partied with high profile people, you partied differently. Everything was smoothing and more elegant. You didn't see the same type of people. You also got the sense that everyone had money.

"This is really nice," I couldn't help but to say to Andrea as we followed the bottle girl to our table. I was looking around trying to take everything in. I looked up at the fancy golden chandeliers.

"I know," she agreed. "And have you looked around at some of the people in here? I mean damn, it feels like I'm at an awards show or something."

"I know what you mean,' I replied.

I spotted a couple of people that I'd only ever seen on tv. There we a couple of rappers and some athletes as well. They were in various VIP sections all around the party. Of course a lot of them had flocks of women trying to get to them, but they seemed to be enjoying themselves.

"Alright ladies, this is your table right here," said the bottle girl as she showed us to our seats. "Give us a couple of minutes and we'll bring you your champagne and a couple of glasses.

"Thanks," I said as Andrea and I both took a seat. I got comfortable as I took in more of the ambiance of the room. I just couldn't get over how beautiful it was. While scanning the room I ended up spotting that guy from the other night, Dylan. I'd thought he was cute from before but since his section was a little closer to mine and I could see him better, I knew how good he actually looked.

CHAPTER 6

Dylan

"Ha, look at this nigga," I said to myself as I drove and slowed down as I reached my destination. It was Friday, the day that Derrick was set to arrive back in Miami with his girlfriend. I decided that I'd go pick him up. I'd cleared my schedule for the day so that we'd have a chance to chill out with one another since we hadn't seen each other in a while.

Derrick had always done well as far as school was concerned. He'd gotten good grades for most of his life and had always known that he wanted to go to college. When a chance for him to stay school longer for a summer internship came up, he took it. I offered to pay for an apartment or something for him for the summer, but the school ended up paying for his room and board while he worked for them. I was proud of my brother for doing his own thing. I hadn't seen him in a few months because of the internship so I was hype to see my only brother in the world.

I decided to go and pick them up on my own. I could have had Slim or Ty come with me or something but I didn't want to make it awkward or anything like that. As I made my way down the road, I couldn't help but to smile a little bit. I hadn't realized until then how much I missed him. My brother was my heart and one of the only people that I felt I could really be myself around. Plus, he didn't judge me for doing my dirt in the streets. He just always warned me to be careful. I knew he looked up to me and didn't want anything to happen to me. He was my only real connection to our mother besides my memories.

I pulled the car up right in front of him but he must not have known it was me because he didn't make any moves towards the car. He was standing there with his phone in his hand, no doubt about to call me because he probably thought I was late or something like that. I realized then that the last time he'd been in town I hadn't been driving this car. I rolled down the tinted window on the jet black four door and leaned my head over a little bit so he could see me.

"You look lost nigga!" I joked. He turned his head down and saw me. He broke into a grin as I climbed out of the car to greet him.

"Damn D, you lost weight or something like that? Your head looks a lot bigger than last time," Derrick joked. He came into me for a handshake that turned into a hug. "Look at you looking like a hood Uber driver."

My brother looked like me without looking like me all at the same time. We both had the same chocolate brown skin but he was a little lighter than I was. The shapes of our faces were the same but his still had some baby weight on it. He was about an inch or so shorter than me but it looked like he'd been working out so he was almost as big.

"Whatever nigga. I don't say nothing about that dome on your head 'cause it'd hurt your feelings," I countered as we broke the hug. I couldn't help but to joke with him. It was what we always did when we got around one another.

Derrick took a step back and motioned for the woman who'd been standing by him to step forward. I had to admit that she was pretty. She had smooth coconut brown skin and jet black curly, natural hair. She was a little slim for my taste, but she definitely had some curves. He'd done well.

"Bro, this is my girl. Naomi, this is Derrick," he introduced us. She smiled politely and reached out for my hand which I took.

"What's up? Nice to meet you. How'd you end up with this one?" I asked playfully.

"We met in ethics class one day and I couldn't get rid of him. We're not together for real but he keeps following me everywhere I go," she said in a serious tone. I looked at Derrick and he and Naomi both busted out laughing.

"I'm joking," she smiled. "We did meet in ethics class a couple of months ago and we've been cool ever since. I like your brother a lot."

"Nice to hear," I said. I reached down and started grabbing their bags to help put them into the trunk. After they were all loaded up, all three of us climbed into my car. Derrick and Naomi sat in the back while I played chauffeur in the front.

I pulled off from the airport and started to drive away. "So, there's been a little change of plans," I announced.

"What happened?" Derrick asked. "Don't tell me you're not going to that party. I was looking forward to it."

I shook my head as we met each other's eyes in the rearview mirror. "Nah, we're *definitely* still going to the party. But I was thinking that after lunch we'd just go back to my spot and y'all could stay there."

Derrick laughed to himself but didn't say anything out loud.

"What happened?" I asked.

"I already knew you were gonna do that," he said with a smile. "It's cool, I missed you too."

I scoffed but didn't say anything else. I wasn't always the best when it came to sharing how I felt with people so I wasn't about to get all mushy and gushy with him. I couldn't lie and say I hadn't missed him though. I wanted him to stay with me at my spot so we'd have more time with one another.

I took Derrick and Naomi out to lunch so I could catch up with him and get to know her. It was cool to do the whole family thing and not have to think about business stuff. My phone went off a few times but unless Slim called, I didn't plan on answering it. I'd told him to only call if it was an emergency since I knew I'd be busy with my brother. Everything would be fine while I enjoyed their company. I'd see him a little later on when he came to my spot for the party. He was coming along with us.

Lunch had been cool. I planned on telling Derrick that Naomi seemed like a solid girl for him. She was in his same year at school and it seemed like she had a good head on her shoulders. Plus, she really seemed to like Derrick and wasn't about trying to run his pockets or anything like that. I as naturally protective of him but so far nothing that Naomi said or did made it seem like she had any ill intentions.

We headed back to my spot and all of us took naps after I got them set up in the guest bedroom. A couple of hours later, all three of us were dressed and ready for the big party on the island.

I wasn't about to put on a full suit or anything like that, but I'd definitely put on something a little fancier than my day to day clothes. I'd bought some new shit the other day so I went through that and pulled something together. I had on gray, slim fit pants with no socks and red bottom loafers. My shirt was white but had a design on it. I also put on a blazer just to be a little more formal.

Derrick and Naomi stepped out looking like a nice, young couple. They were each wearing purple: her a purple dress and him a purple, slim fit suit with a black shirt underneath. Slim was already downstairs waiting for us alongside one of our other boys, Tyrell, who was also coming with us.

I'd rented a car for the night, a big body Range Rover. If we were going to the party, we were showing up in style. Derrick and his girl both seemed impressed with everything as Tyrell drove us to the party.

"Dylan, what's this party for?" Derrick asked from the back.

I shrugged my shoulders. "Who knows? You

know how rich niggas are. They'll throw a party for everything and nothing all at the same time. I think it's just the opening of the new private club but I'm not sure."

"Oh, alright cool," he said. "Who's supposed to be there?"

"You got a lot of questions for a nigga that getting in for free," I joked. He joined me in laughter. "It's definitely an A-list event. Top of the line people, so I imagine we'll see some people we know."

The night air was warm as we stepped out of the car. I could hear music playing from somewhere but wasn't sure if it was coming from the club or one of the expensive houses on the island. I'd gone ahead and added Derrick and Naomi's names to the RSVP for the party after he told me they were coming. I also got us moved into a bigger VIP section since there was more of us. Like I said, when I went out, I liked to go *out*. I laughed whenever I saw a big group of people all crowding around one or two little bottles that they were trying to savor it for along as possible. Niggas needed to step their weight up.

Once we got inside, I had to admit to

myself that the spot was a nice one, probably one of the nicest that I'd been to. It didn't seem like they'd spared any money when it came to it. I looked around and spotted a couple of hustlers and people that I knew. I also saw a couple of athletes and other high-profile people. I knew a couple of them from around the city, so I made a mental note to go and make my rounds after I'd been there for a little bit.

We'd been at the party for a little over half an hour and it was fun. The crowd was definitely high energy and it seemed like everyone was trying their hardest to have a good time. It wasn't hard to do either. The DJ had the place jumping. There was liquor flowing everywhere and they kept announcing the dance and best dressed contests that were happening later.

Derrick and his girl were out on the dance floor doing their thing. Slim was letting some chick sweet talk him, whispering in his ear and all that. I was scoping out the crowd when I noticed these two chicks walk into the room. Both of them were bad but the one in the green dress was on some next level shit. I wasn't thirsty or anything, but I was definitely watching them.

They got seated in a VIP section not too far away from mine.

I turned to Slim and tapped him on the shoulder to get him away from the chick in his ear.

"What?" he asked as he leaned into me.

"Yo, you know who they are? They shorty in the green over there?" I asked as I pointed towards where the two girls were seated. "I ain't never seen them before."

He put his hand on his chin to think for a second. "I seen shorty before. She works over at um...Club Tease. I seen her dance a couple of times. She's top quality. She made it rain in there bro. Shit, I even gave her a card one time and told her she should come dance at one of your clubs."

"She bad as shit," I said. I flagged down one of the waiters by waving my hands to get his attention. He walked over to me after making his way through the crowd.

"How can I help you?" he asked loudly over the music.

"Yo, check this out," I said as I stood up to lean into his ear. "You see that table over there with those two women? I want you to take another bottle of champagne over there. Matter of fact, all of their drinks for the rest of the night are on my tab. Make sure they know it's on me. Cool?" I knew one way to get someone's attention when I wanted it.

"No problem sir," the waiter said before he walked off.

CHAPTER 7

Alivia

"Fuck it up!" I yelled as I laughed. Andrea was standing up and twerking to the song that was almost over. We'd been at the private club for a good little minute and I was enjoying myself. The music was everything. The champagne was flowing and the crowd was lit.

Andrea and I hadn't hit the dance floor but the two of us had been having our own good time right in our little VIP section. A couple of dudes had come over to try and talk to us or get us to dance, but we'd shut them down. They seemed like lames.

Andrea had just sat down when a bottle girl came over to us with another bottle of champagne.

"You order that?" I asked Andrea. She shook her head. "Me either."

The bottle girl put the champagne into the ice bucket next to the other almost empty bottle. "This is from the guy over there at table 7," she explained as she pointed. "He says that you guys' drinks are covered by him all night. Let me know if you need anything else." She turned and walked away after.

Andrea and I exchanged a look. We reached down and poured ourselves two glasses of the new bottle. I couldn't front; I was definitely impressed. Guys could sometimes act like buying someone a drink during a happy hour was something major. This dude had sent us an entire bottle of champagne, *and* was covering our drinks for the night.

We both turned towards the guy and held up our glasses towards him. I mouthed "thank you" since I knew he wouldn't be able to hear me if I yelled from where I was. He played it cool, nodding back at us before he turned his attention back to the people in his section. I'd locked eyes with him for a second. It felt intense.

"Damn girl, he was eyeing you," Andrea said.

"Was he?" I asked with a little smile. "He's cute."

"Bitch, cute is for puppy dogs and babies. Than man is attractive," she laughed. "He must not have seen you the other night at the club, but he's *definitely* noticed you here."

"What else you know about him?" I asked. Andrea had been able to tell me a little about him the other night but nothing too much. It was obvious that he was a baller. His outfit was on point without it looking like it was trying to be. He had a nice little entourage with him and judging by the women trying to get into his section, he had money. I already knew that though. I'd pepped how he'd been buying bottles and stuff all night long.

"Not much," she said. "He's from the hood though. I know that much. What you gonna do?"

I shrugged casually. "Who knows? I'm not gonna think about it. I'm just gonna have a good time and see how the night goes."

We kept on partying until they announced that it was time for the best dressed contest. Andrea and I were both excited so when they made the announcement, we both made our way to the stage.

There was a good couple of girls lined up. It was a little shady though because the main competition was on the stage but if you didn't look right, they wouldn't let you get that far. There was this one fat chick with a bad weave who they turned away before she even got to the stairs leading to the stage.

The guy doing the contest was doing it Apollo style and letting the crowd cheer and vote for who they wanted. Andrea and I both got a chance to show off our dresses and do a little catwalk across the stage. I took my time doing my sexy walk and making eye contact with as many people as I could. Andrea got a lot of applause but mine was definitely louder.

I thought for sure that I was the winner until this white bitch came to the stage. She was some basic chick with huge fake breasts and an ass that she clearly hadn't been born with either. She hit the stage and started doing all this weird dancing and stuff like she was in a pageant. Her breasts "accidentally" popped out of her dress at one point. I don't know what kind of accident it was, but it definitely took her a while to put them back inside. When the crowd cheered for her, you could hear all the thirsty ass niggas in the room yelling and whooping for her. She ended up coming in first, while me and Andrea came in second and third respectively.

The white girl got $500 while I got $250 and Andrea $100. We took our money and made our way back over to the VIP. I was glad that we hadn't finished that champagne because I wanted to celebrate my win. I didn't mind coming in second because I knew that the white chick only won because of her cheap trick. Either way, coming in second and third out of all the girls who'd been competing wasn't anything to be mad about.

We'd only been back at our section for a couple of minutes when I felt someone tap me on the shoulder. I turned around to see this tall, brown skinned dude behind us.

"Yes?" I asked. I didn't want to come across as rude but I wasn't in the mood to dance.

"Yo, my boy asked me to come over to congratulate y'all," he said. He nodded his head in the direction of the guy who'd sent us the champagne. "He wanted to know if y'all wanted to join him for a drink to celebrate."

Andrea and I could communicate without saying anything. We exchanged a quick look before I answered the guy.

"Yeah, no problem. We'll be over in a few minutes," I said. I wasn't about to get up and rush over there. We'd look thirsty. It would be best if we just played it cool and went over at our own pace. We drank a little bit more of the champagne and then made our way over to their section.

The guy who'd bought the champagne stood as we got over to them. I felt his eyes on me as I got closer. With him and I finally being so close to one another, I was able to fully take him in. He looked as good as I'd assumed he would in person. He also smelled good which was always a bonus.

"What's good? My name's Dylan," he introduced himself in a deep voice. He extended his hand.

I reached out and grabbed it. "I'm Alivia," I said. "This is my best friend, Andrea." She smiled at him and shook his hand.

He took a moment to introduce us to everyone he was with: his brother and his girl-friend, and two of his friends. The two of us joined them sitting on the couch. They made sure to offer us drinks, which we accepted, and got into a conversation.

"You know, you guys should have won that contest," Dylan commented. "That white bitch got nothing on you." His eyes scanned my body and lingered on my breasts.

"Word," his friend Slim chimed in. It was clear that he was feeling Andrea. I wasn't sure if she noticed but he was definitely scooting himself closer to her. He'd been talking to some chick all night, but he dismissed her as soon as we got over there. She must not have been too hurt though because she'd moved on to the dude who'd come over to get us from our section.

"It's whatever. It was just something to do for fun," I said to Dylan.

He shook his head. "Nah, I'm serious. You

the baddest thing in the club. Ain't no way you should've lost."

I didn't know if it was the liquor or the fact that I was becoming more and more attracted to him, but I suddenly felt like I could listen to Dylan talk all night long.

CHAPTER 8

Dylan

I was playing it cool on the outside but in my head, I couldn't deny that Alivia was definitely something else. Seeing her up close and person, I understood what Slim had been talking about. She looked better than every other chick in there and she was fully dressed. I could only imagine what she looked like at the strip club with all her clothes off, but I planned on hopefully seeing that for myself.

"How'd you hear about this place?" I asked her.

"This guy I met through work invited me," she said. She looked around. "Funnily enough, I haven't even seen him tonight. Not that I was looking. What about you?"

"I get invited to stuff like this all the time," I said coolly. "I'm glad I came to this one though." I licked my lips at her and she blushed a little bit."

"So where's your nigga at?" I went on. I knew that she hadn't come in there with anyone besides her friend. Hell, she'd turned down every other dude that had even approached her to dance. "He let you come out looking good like that ain't even bother to show up with you?"

"If I had a man, I'd still look this good." She laughed a little bit. Damn, she had some beautiful teeth. "I'm single," she responded. She held up her left hand in a dramatic way. "No rings and ain't nobody hitting my line like that either. What about you? I peeped the way the birds flocked over here after y'all arrived."

"Yeah, they all tried to get in here but look who I'm sitting next to," I shot back. I knew I was running game on her but it seemed to be working. I could tell by her body language that she was opening up to me. "Maybe we can kick it tonight take it from there."

"We'll see," she said with a smirk. "I wanted

to thank you again for the champagne and the drinks. I appreciate it."

"It's nothing to me, baby. But I'm glad you like it," I said. "So can I be honest with you?"

She nodded her head. "Well shit, I hope didn't plan on lying to me since we just met," she joked.

I joined her in laughter and moved a little closer to her on the couch. "Not trying to embarrass you or anything like that, but one of my boys recognized you from the strip club, Tease?"

She was staring me in the eye and didn't blink as she answered. "Nothing for me to be embarrassed about. Yeah, I work there. Everybody has their hustle. What's yours?"

She had some fire inside of her and I liked it. "All hustles are my hustles," I stated. "I don't brag about mine but trust me, my pockets are always good."

"Good pockets are one thing, but is your life on track?" she questioned me. I honestly hadn't been expecting something like that, so it caught me off guard.

"It's all good," I replied.

"I feel you," she said. "So, are you from Miami?"

"Hell yeah," I said proudly. "Born and raised. I ain't one of these new niggas who just moved down here for the clout or the beach. What about you?"

"Yeah, I grew up in the projects. I should have known you were from down here. You've got the look," she said. She got a thoughtful look on her face before she asked me her next question. "So why'd you buy me and my friend that champagne?"

It was my turn to smirk. "Why do you think I bought it?"

"'Cause you wanted my attention," she said as she sipped her drinks.

I shook my head, still smirking at her. I whispered in her ear and slipped my hand onto her thigh. "I could've bought you one drink to get your attention. I bought the bottle so I could *keep* your attention. How's that sound?"

I could tell that Alivia was impressed with my answer and me in general. The more we talked, the more into me she seemed to be. I could tell from our little conversation right there on the couch that she had a good head on her shoulders. She might have been a stripper but it seemed like she had more class than a lot of professional women that I knew. The gears of my mind were already working and I was already thinking about keeping her. Hell, she could be my main kept bitch.

Alivia and I kept on talking for a little while longer. Everything was going cool until one of the bottle girls came over with two other girls behind her. I had to admit that they were pretty, but still on the basic side. Nice bodies on both of 'em, but it was all fake. They were strippers. Slim had found out that we could get lap dances and had asked for them.

It was a little reckless, but they ended up giving us lap dances right there at the table. Neither of them took any clothes off but they did their thing. One of them danced on me and the other on Slim. I wished that we'd canceled it since we had Alivia and her friend with us now but we just went with it. They both sat there and watched us get our dances.

When they'd finished up, I gave each of them $50 a piece and sent them on their way. I sat down next to Alivia. She'd been quiet while I was getting the dance. I looked at her in the face. Her eyes were a little low from the liquor but the look on her face definitely showed she had a little attitude. I hoped I hadn't been wrong about me thinking she was cool.

"You good?" I asked.

"No," she answered.

"What? You not bugging out over the lap dance right?" Damn, if she was about to give me a headache already, I'd be sending her back to her own section. I hoped she wasn't about on trip on me or anything like that.

"Yeah," she said as she stood up. I thought she was about to leave but she turned to me instead. "I hate a bitch that can't give a lap dance the right way. Let me give you a *real* one and show you how it's done."

At that point my little smirk turned into a smile. "Oh word?" I got comfortable on the couch and leaned back a little bit, folding both of my hands and putting them behind my head. I wanted to see what she had to show me.

Alivia didn't say another word as she started to dance. It almost felt like she had some kind of magic or something like that. She kept her eyes locked on me the entire time that she danced, never taking her eyes off of me. It felt like everything and everyone else in the place faded away.

I was focused on her and her body. She wasn't moving to the music, at least not the music that the DJ was playing. Her hips, ass, and legs all moved at their own pace as though she was playing something in her head. She was slow and seductive with the way that she moved. Every move was well thought out. She might have been wearing this elegant dress and all, but it was clear that she wasn't about to let that stop her from giving me the dance.

I knew that other people had to be looking at us. Our VIP section was a little elevated on a platform so I knew that plenty of people could see us. I didn't give a fuck. Actually, I liked the attention. Every nigga in the club could want her but it was clear that Alivia was moving for me and me alone.

Slowly and seductively she began to back her body onto mine, lowering her hips and ass onto my lap. If I was some lame dude then I might have been on brick or something but I played it cool. I didn't know if she always gave out dances like the one that she was giving me but if she did, I could see why my boy had given her a card to try and come work at one of my clubs. She was obvious a top draw. By the time she'd finished it felt like she'd fulfilled all my fantasies and I hadn't even touched her once.

Alivia finished her dance with a slow and sexy whine down to the couch. She crossed her legs in front of her like she hadn't done anything at all. Little did she know that her dance had low key been an audition. Not for the club but for me. By the time she'd finished making her moves, I knew that I had to have her. I needed to keep her. I was determined to make that happen by any means.

CHAPTER 9

Alivia

The private club was on tilt and I was lit up. The liquor had been flowing freely like water all night long and needless to say, I was feeling it. I always tried to carry myself with class, so I wasn't the type to drink and get sloppy. Still, I was buzzed, maybe a little beyond buzzed. I got up right there in the middle of the club and did an elaborate lap dance for Dylan, so I knew I was probably more far gone than I believed myself to be. He enjoyed it though. Once I had finished and sat down next to him, my eyes locked onto Andrea. She gave me a smirk and a slight nod of approval before she kept on talking to Dylan's friend Slim.

I knew that at some point Andrea and I planned on going back to our own section, but we never ended up making it. The atmosphere in the club was everything. We'd been having fun on our own but we were having more fun with Dylan and his people. I was glad that Dylan's brother's girlfriend was cool and not intimidated by us. The guys all made fun of us because Naomi, Andrea, and I all hit the dance floor, tipsy as hell, and danced with one another. I was feeling it though.

After some time, it was clear that the party was starting to die down. A good amount of people had already started to leave. The DJ was playing a lot of those "end of party" songs to start to usher people out of the private club. Andrea had driven her car to the party. Before we'd even gotten there we were trying to figure out what to do if we were tipsy by the end of the night. I asked her if she was good to drive and she said yeah. The two of us stood up and were about to leave when Dylan stood up to.

"Damn, you were just gonna leave without saying anything?" Dylan was standing so close to me that I could feel the heat radiating off of him. The smell of his expensive cologne was all up my nose. I looked at his full lips and wondered what it would be like to kiss them, or have them other places on me.

I giggled. "All I did was stand up. I hadn't gone anywhere yet," I replied.

"So what are y'all about to do?" Dylan asked. He licked his lips slowly and then ran his eyes across my body. He knew what he was doing to me. "The night doesn't have to end right now."

"We were planning on going home. What are *y'all* about to do?"

"Why don't we got back to my crib and relax? A little after party situation? Maybe a few drinks or something like that," Dylan said. It was clear that he was smooth talker and he knew it too. I hadn't planned on meeting anyone at the club or anything but Dylan was...different. I loved the energy that he gave off. He carried himself like a boss and wasn't afraid to show off his power. I could tell that he and his friends were really cool but he was definitely in charge

I looked at Andrea, who was smiling all in

Slim's face. I could have asked for her opinion, but I already knew what she was going to say. "We can do that," I said. "How about we follow you guys since we drove?"

A smile crept up on Dylan's face. It was clear that this was his plan the whole time. "Alright, sounds good. Let's go."

Our little crew all made our way outside the private club. There were a couple more valets there than before. They were moving as fast as they could to get everyone their cars. Dylan's brother, Derrick, and his girlfriend ended up taking a cab back home. Dylan mentioned earlier in the day that they were staying with him, so I didn't understand why they weren't going to the same place as us. Dylan said that we were going to another one of his spots while they were going back to his house. I was tipsy and didn't feel like asking anymore questions, so I just let it go.

Once everyone had gotten their cars and keys back, we climbed into our vehicles and started driving. Andrea rolled the windows down to try and sober up a little bit. I didn't like driving with people who'd been drinking, but I'd been in the car with her more times than I could count, so I knew it was safe.

"Girl, how did we get here?" I asked as I busted out laughing. Andrea did too. "I was just coming to have a good time."

"Shit, you tell me. You were the one who got us over there," she replied. "You worked your magic on Dylan and now he don't wanna let you go."

"I didn't do anything to that man," I said. "He must be feeling me though to be sending us bottles and shit."

"Right," she agreed. "So, what was up with that lap dance?"

"What?" I asked in an innocent voice. "I was just doing my job. I give lap dances and that was a lap dance."

Andrea laughed again. "That wasn't the club. You put it all the way on him and now he doesn't wanna let you go. Shit, you better be giving him some pussy tonight before he starts stalking you at the club.

I shrugged. "We'll see how this little night cap goes. I can't front though, I'm enjoying the vibe."

"Me too," Andrea agreed. "Slim was whispering all kinds of shit in my ear all night. He's got me a little hot and bothered."

"I know the feeling," I said. "At least they're not corny."

"Word," she agreed.

We followed the guys for a couple more minutes until we finally pulled up in a quiet neighborhood. It was clearly still the city but it wasn't any of the main parts of Miami. They showed us where we could park and then waited for us to get out of the car.

I was impressed by everything that I saw. The building itself was incredibly nice. We rode the elevator upstairs to almost the top floor. Dylan opened the door to the apartment and I almost gasped.

Andrea and I lived in what I thought was a big apartment, but it seemed like most of it could fit into the living room of that place. It was decorated in a very manly way with lots of black, white, and silver. It was clear that no amount of money had been spared when it came to decoration. I noticed top of the line everything.

"This place is really nice," I commented as I

walked in. My heels were clicking loudly on the hardwood floor.

"Thanks," Dylan said humbly. "I try to keep everything I have looking nice. Y'all take a seat on the couch while I fix us a couple of drinks. Anything in particular?"

Andrea and I sat down on the couch while Slim sat in one of the armchairs. Dylan walked over to the little bar section of his spot.

"You got any champagne?" I asked. I was already tipsy enough and didn't need to be getting drunk and sloppy on top of it. Dylan looked in the little fridge that held some of his liquor and pulled out a bottle of expensive champagne.

"You don't have to open it up for me. That's expensive," I said.

Dylan shrugged. "I got three more of 'em. Fuck it. Let's drink." He turned towards the kitchen and pushed the cork on the bottle with his thumb until it shot off and hit the wall on the other side of the room.

He pulled out four glasses and started to pour. Andrea and Slim were already giving each other the "come fuck me" look so I wanted to get away from them. I stood up and walked over to Dylan.

"I came to help you with the drinks," I said.

Now that we were outside the club atmosphere and things calmed down, I could really feel Dylan out and see what he was about. I knew that I was feeling him already and he didn't have to say anything back to let me know that he was thinking the same. I guess what I was trying to figure out next was whether this was going to be a one-night kind of thing or something more serious. I guessed that only time would tell but for the moment I just planned on enjoying the vibe.

"Oh word?" He smirked at me. "What else can you help me with?" He raised his eyebrow at me in a sexy way as his eyes lingered on my body again. I was feeling that same warmth that I'd felt earlier.

"I got a couple of ideas," I flirted back. I grabbed two of the glasses from the counter and turned to take one of them back to Andrea. I was doing a slow and sexy walk. I didn't even have to turn around to know that his eyes were all on me. "If you play your cards right."

"I like the sound of that," Dylan flirted

back. His eyes were a little low from the alcohol, but I could see lust inside of them. "Maybe I could get another dance or something…"

"Why do that when you could have the real thing?" I teased. I grabbed two of the glasses and took them into the living room followed by Dylan.

The four of us sat around on Dylan's couches and chilled out for a little bit. We talked about the club and all the people who were there. We also recapped the dance and best dressed contest. It was really nice to just sit and talk with the guys for a little bit. Dylan ended up turning on some music from the expensive speakers in the living room. It was that weird part of the night where it was almost morning but the sun had barely started to rise. There was a Quiet Storm radio mix on. It was playing all the smooth throwback 90's and early 2000's R&B. it was definitely perfect for the mood that we were in.

We sat around talking about the party for a little bit longer until it seemed like we were running out of topics. We commented on all the celebrities that we'd seen and stuff like that. After a while though it became clear that we were ready to partner off and take the party somewhere else. The conversation was starting to die down. Dylan was sitting next to me on the couch with my hand in his. His finger kept caressing the top of my hand and I kept noticing him sneaking glances at me. When Andrea got up and moved to the same armchair as Slim, I figured it would be time for us to go somewhere else too.

"Did you decorate this place yourself?" I asked Dylan.

He shrugged. "Kind of. I worked with an interior designer and pretty much told her what I wanted. She picked out a lot of it but I liked it."

"Did she decorate *all* the rooms?" I asked. I hoped he was getting what I was trying to say to him.

Dylan's eyes got a little wide and then he smirked. "Yeah. I could show 'em to you if you want. A little tour."

"That would be nice," I said. I looked at Andrea, who clearly wasn't paying any attention to us. I halfway mumbled that I'd be back after Dylan showed me his spot, but she just waved her hand and said alright.

Dylan took me by the hand and led me through his apartment. There wasn't really much else to see. The living room and kitchen were open and right next to one another. There was only one bedroom and it was decorated similarly to the living room but with more gray. The bed was extra big, probably a King sized. It looked big and comfortable.

Dylan turned around to face me and took a step towards me. He was breathing a little heavy as he looked at me. "So, what you think?" he asked. His voice was slow and deep as he spoke.

"I like what I see," I said.

"Me too," he replied.

Dylan leaned his head down and did what I'd been wanting him to do for the last few hours. His perfectly full lips first brushed against mine before he applied more pressure and turned it into a full-blown kiss. It was passionate, much more passionate than I was expecting it to be. He put one of his hands on my face and the other was rubbing my back over the material of the dress.

I reached behind me and slowly unzipped the dress. Dylan unclasped the part at the top that was still holding it up. It ended up falling to the floor at my ankles. We never broke the kiss, but Dylan's eyes opened as he looked at my body. I was as naked as the day I was born, minus the gold heels that I was still wearing.

"You're so fucking sexy," Dylan broke the kiss and whispered in my ear. He licked and sucked at my ear lobe for a couple of seconds. It was like he already knew my body because that was definitely one of my spots.

He moved with control as he stepped away from me. Dylan unbuttoned his shirt and dropped it on the ground. His body was even better than I thought it would be. It was clear that he took his workouts serious. He looked like some kind of African God or something like that with his smooth brown skin and muscles. He took another step back until he was on the bed. He pushed himself back some more and propped himself up on his elbows. I looked down at the pants he was wearing and saw something thick starting to poke through. He used his finger to tell me to come over.

I was still feeling my liquor, but I was more intoxicated by him. I slowly and sexily walked over to him like someone straight out of a porn or something. I let my ponytail down and my hair fell down across my shoulders. I got to the bed and climbed on top of it, and then Dylan, straddling him.

"Damn yo," Dylan said. He took a moment to admire my body. His firm hands rubbed all over me, gripping my ass, waist and breasts as though I was clay and he was trying to mold me into something else. "You look so good."

His hands were playing with both of my nipples as I leaned down and started kissing him again, this time more aggressively than before. The room was dark but the curtains were open and the moonlight was shining through. I could make out the look of ecstasy on his face as we kissed.

I moved my body like a snake as I lowered myself down his body. I undid his belt and everything with a little help from him. I stood up to pull his pants down.

"Wow," I commented. With his pants all the way off, Dylan slipped out of his underwear and was slowly massaging his dick to its full potential. It was thick as hell.

"If you like it why don't you touch it?" Dylan said. He knew what he was working with and he was cocky about it, no pun intended.

I didn't say anything to him as I locked my eyes on him and took it into my hand. I started to massage it myself and then jerk it up and down, never breaking my eye contact with him. A couple of seconds later I bent my head down and started to give him head. He was the one who lost our little staring contest because after a short while, he was moaning and throwing his head back. I knew my head game was top of the line and he was proving it to me.

"Oh shit," he moaned. He reached above his head and grabbed a pillow. I guess he didn't want to be too loud in case Andrea and Slim heard us, but I was sure that they were out there doing their own thing. "Slob that shit."

I was humming and moaning as my head went up and down on his dick. I didn't know when the last time he'd had some pussy was but it couldn't have been any time recent. He was completely brick like it'd been some time.

"I wanna taste you," Dylan said. I'd been giving him head for a good couple of minutes and I could tell by how he was moving that he was close to his orgasm. He hadn't brought me all the way to his spot just to get some head.

I stood all the way up and then climbed into

the bed. I was going to go further back on it but Dylan told me to stay at the edge. He stood up and walked in front of me, kneeling down on the carpet at he did. From the way that he propped my legs up on his shoulders, I knew that he was about to go to work.

Dylan buried himself in my pussy face first. It was always funny when it came to dudes like him. A lot of dudes always made a big show out of the things that they didn't do but behind closed doors, they ate pussy and ass just like everyone else. I didn't know how many people he'd done it to, but it was clear that Dylan knew his way around a vagina. He was a little rough as he worked his tongue in and out of me but that only turned me on more. He was licking and sucking at my inner thighs too which were really sensitive in a good way.

"Ooh," I moaned loudly. I grabbed the pillow that he moved and put it over my face to drown out my moans, and there were a lot of them.

"Oh shit," I moaned again. I put my hand on the back of Dylan's head and pushed him further into me.

"You taste good yo," Dylan said as he briefly came up for air. "So fuckin' good."

He put his hand on the middle of my chest and pushed me back a little bit. He pulled his head out from between my legs and then went over to the nightstand. He came back with a condom that he tore open and slid onto himself.

I was still lying there feeling amazing from the head that he'd given me. I raised my legs in the air and he gripped them, putting them onto either of his shoulders while I lay on my back. He maneuvered his body to line itself up with mine and slowly started to push himself inside of me.

"Mmm," I moaned as the thick head went in. He took his time, slowly pushing himself into me inch by inch until he was all the way inside.

"You got some good ass pussy," Dylan grunted as he started working himself in and out of me. He spread my legs open a little more so that he could really get himself inside. After a couple of minutes, he'd built up speed and rhythm.

"Fuck me," I moaned. Dylan leaned down and started licking and sucking on my breasts. He'd stop every now and then to kiss me.

"You like this dick?" he asked as he pounded away at me.

"Yeah," I cooed. I was loving every stroke. Dylan knew what he was doing and it was driving me crazy. My body was warm and tingly all over.

"This my pussy now, right?" he questioned me. When I didn't answer fast enough he started to stroke me deeper and harder. "This mine, right?"

"Mmm, hmm, yeah," I moaned. I reached up and started grabbing at his back to pull him more into me. My body shook as I orgasmed.

"Ahh shit!" Dylan let out a loud groan a few minutes later. I felt his whole body go rigid and then limp as he fell onto the bed next to me breathing just as deeply as I was.

After all the drinking, partying, and then the sex on top of it, needless to say we were exhausted. Dylan and I had just enough energy to clean up and climb under the covers on his soft bed. He pulled me closer to him and I ended up falling asleep right there on his chest.

Waking up the next morning, it took me a couple of seconds to remember where I was. I sat up in the bed and looked around. I realized that Dylan wasn't there and neither were his clothes. I was about to go into the living room and look for Andrea when I realized that he'd left a note on the pillow that he'd slept on.

I had to go and take care of a couple of things. You and your girl can see yourselves out. Feel free to eat and drink what you want before you dip out. I had a good time with you. Everything that we saw and did last night could be yours if you're willing to be mine.

-D

I read through the note a couple of times before I got out of the bed. "So you want me to be yours, huh?" I said out loud as I grabbed my dress from the floor.

CHAPTER 10

Dylan

"Yo bro, how was it with that Andrea chick last night?" I asked Slim. The two of us were in my car. We'd just left out the condo and were heading back to my house. I told Derrick and Jasmine I'd meet up with them later in the day for dinner but I wanted to stop and change my clothes and everything first.

Slim got this stupid grin on his face. "She knew what she was doing," he said. "I'd been whispering all kinds of shit to her in the club and she was with it. It's cool when they don't front about liking sex. We all do."

"Word," I agreed. "I'm feeling Alivia for

real." Slim and I were the best of friends, so I never felt the need to hide things from him. I was telling the truth about Alivia. I didn't know what it was about her but she definitely had me open. I wanted to get to know her better and I definitely needed to lock her down before she got away from me.

"I would be too if she put on a show like the one she did last night," Slim said.

I couldn't help but to laugh. "Shit, you saw that?" I asked. The lap dance that she'd given me was something that I hadn't expected but was incredibly open to. I owned a few strip clubs so it wasn't like I hadn't had a chick come and dance for me. Alivia moved like she'd made the moves herself. Her body was everything and she hit every beat. If we hadn't been in the middle of the club, I probably would have tried to fuck her right there.

Slim joined me in laughter. "The whole club was watching. When we were leaving I heard a couple of dudes talking about how she'd turned them down for dances all night."

"She's definitely something serious," I stated. "With the way we were carrying on I thought y'all heard us out in the living room."

He shook his head and smirked. "Nope. We were too busy making our own noises." We both laughed.

Slim and I had some business to handle. He dropped me at my crib to shower and change and said he'd be back in a few after he did the same. When I got upstairs I couldn't help but to laugh. It looked like Derrick and Jasmine had a night similar to mine. Their clothes were all in the living room and I assumed they were in the bedroom still sleeping.

I didn't plan on waking them up so I went into my master bedroom to shower and change. I put my clothes from the night before on top of the dresser so I'd remember to send them to the dry cleaners later on. I realized before I got in the shower that I could still smell Alivia's scent all over me. I hadn't been lying to her a couple of hours earlier when I said she had some good pussy. It felt like I could swim in it.

About an hour later, Slim and I were driving to Little Haiti to meet up with Jean to finalize the plans for the next drop. We got to the little house that he lived in and hopped outside. I never liked going to that part of the city. It always felt like we were being watched when we were there. I knew we were safe as long as we stayed cool with Jean and his brother though.

We knocked on the door and an older woman ended up opening it up. I'd been to Jean's house a few times. It always looked like he was trying to give off this old school mob boss vibe. His usually did all of his business at his wooden kitchen table. It seemed like there was a permanent cloud of smoke in the air from someone puffing weed.

We headed into the kitchen where he was seated at the table. He motioned for us to sit down and offered each of us a drink.

"Nah, I'm good," I said. "It's a little early for me."

"Me too. I had enough last night," Slim said. I was glad that neither of us were nursing hangovers. Still, it was probably best not to drink and do business.

"Suit yourselves," Jean said as he took a long sip of the brown liquid and sloshed it around before it put it back on the table. He and his brother were born in the United States but raised primarily in Haiti. As a result, they learned to switch back and forth between their

American and Haitian accents. "So how's this happening this time around?"

"I got a warehouse shipment coming in next week," I said. "A bunch of electronics and stuff. We can do it then."

"In one shipment?" Jean asked. "You sure? You know you like to switch things up."

I nodded my head. "Just the one truck should be fine for this," I responded. "You just make sure your people aren't late like last time."

Jean sucked his teeth. "I know what I'm doing," he shot back. "You just make sure *you're* there when you need to be."

"Not a problem," I said. "The cash will be there too."

"That's all I ask," Jean said with smile.

After we'd finalized the last few details, Slim and I got out of there. We didn't really like to be friendly with Jean because it was just business. He knew that, so he didn't take any offense.

While we drove, I pulled out my phone to make a call. Alivia had given me her number the night before. I texted her right after so that she had mine. It was the middle of the afternoon so I knew that her and her friend had to be home already.

"Hello?" Alivia answered the call.

"Why you sound so surprised? You give your number out like that?" I joked.

"I didn't save it, but I'm doing it now," she said. "How are you?"

"I'm good. What about you? What you up to?" I asked.

"Just handling some business, same as ever," I answered. "So did you have a chance to read my letter?"

"Yeah," she said.

I nodded my head. "So how you feel about it?" I asked. I knew that she'd probably been thinking about it since she read it.

"I think we should talk about it in person," she said.

"Ok cool. That's not a problem. How about you send me your address and I pick you up a little later for dinner?"

"Sounds like a plan," she said. "I'm about to get in the shower but I'll text you my address now. Just let me know what time you'll be here."

"Cool," I said.

A few hours later, Alivia and I were arriving at a restaurant out on South Beach. I was in the mood for Cuban food and knew of a spot with really good dishes. We got a table out on the sidewalk since it was a nice, warm night. That was one thing I could say that I loved about Miami; the weather was almost always perfect.

We ordered food and drinks and made small talk until we got to talking about the main topic. I was curious to see how she felt about everything so far. I also wanted to see how she'd react when I told her what I had in mind.

"So what did you mean in your note?" Alivia asked. She took a sip of her wine and looked me in the eye.

"You know what I meant. I want you to be mine," I said.

"Yeah, but what does that *mean?*" she questioned. "You said everything that we did could be mine. I don't think you're trying to play me or anything like that, but I gotta keep my guard up."

I nodded my head with approval. "I know what you mean. I can tell you got a good head on your shoulders," I said.

"So what's up? Keep it real with me," she challenged.

"Alright," I said, putting my fork down. I

reached into my pocket and handed her a piece of paper. She unfolded it and stared.

"What's this?" she asked.

"I don't do things the way a lot of other people do," I began to explain. "I have my hands in a lot of different things and I can't be too tied down. That's a list of rules you gotta follow if you really wanna fuck with me. I don't want you to get the wrong idea or anything like that. I'm feeling you and if you wanna be mine then I'm gonna put you above everyone else. You gotta be willing to follow my rules though."

Alivia didn't say anything as she looked down at the list I'd written.

"Can we talk about this?" she asked.

"I mean, I can explain them if you want but they're not gonna change," I countered.

She looked down at the paper again and read through the rules out loud. "Quit your job. Make sure the house is clean. Don't question me about coming and going. Always be available on the phone. No spending the night out, and I've gotta let you know who I'm with if you ask. And more."

I simply nodded.

She looked puzzled. "So I can't work? What am I supposed to do for money and stuff?

"You'd be taken care of," I said. "I'd put you up in your own crib. The only people who'd have the key would be you and me. I'd throw you some cash every week and take care of the bills."

She didn't seem sold yet. Even that was something that I liked about her. A lot of these birds out here got really excited whenever someone dangled a dollar in front of them. It was clear that she wasn't one of those people.

"No company?" she asked.

I shook my head. "Nah, not like that. You can have your friends and family over but you know, nothing too crazy or anything like that. Obviously no niggas can come and visit."

"This is a lot," she said.

"Look, I know on paper it sounds like a lot. But think of it this way, it's the same things we'd agree to if we were in a relationship, just on paper. It's not all bad though. It'll honestly make things easier cause this way you won't have to worry about anything. You already know what the deal is," I explained. I sat back in the chair. "So, what you wanna do?"

Alivia took in a deep breath and let it out slowly. "Well, I…"

Find out what happens next in part two of Torn Between A Thug & A Boss! Available Now!

To find out when Mia Black has new books available and to get exclusive free ebooks, **follow Mia Black on Instagram for more updates: @authormiablack**

TORN BETWEEN A THUG & A BOSS 2

Alivia never imagined she'd be a kept woman. It's a lot to get used to and so out of her element. Following Dylan's strict rules and behaving by a code of conduct isn't something she's ever had to do, but it just might be worth it to have the life she's always wanted.

Yet, a vacation to the Bahamas might make their agreement null and void when a meeting with a mysterious man threatens Alivia's new-found lifestyle.

Will she choose to remain true to her word or has she found a new path to follow?

Find out what happens in part two of Torn Between A Thug & Boss!

Made in the USA
Monee, IL
11 February 2020